For Papa,
de scheepstimmerman

· · · ➤✳︎◄ · · ·

First U.S. edition 2014

Library of Congress Catalog Card Number 2013944028
ISBN 978-0-7636-6783-2

14 15 16 17 18 19 SCP 10 9 8 7 6 5 4 3 2

Printed in Humen, Dongguan, China

This book was typeset in Fairfield.
The illustrations were done in watercolor, pencil, and collage.

Candlewick Press
99 Dover Street
Somerville, Massachusetts 02144

visit us at www.candlewick.com

Milo and Millie

Jedda Robaard

CANDLEWICK PRESS

This is Millie and me.

We went on an adventure.

We sailed past a busy city . . .

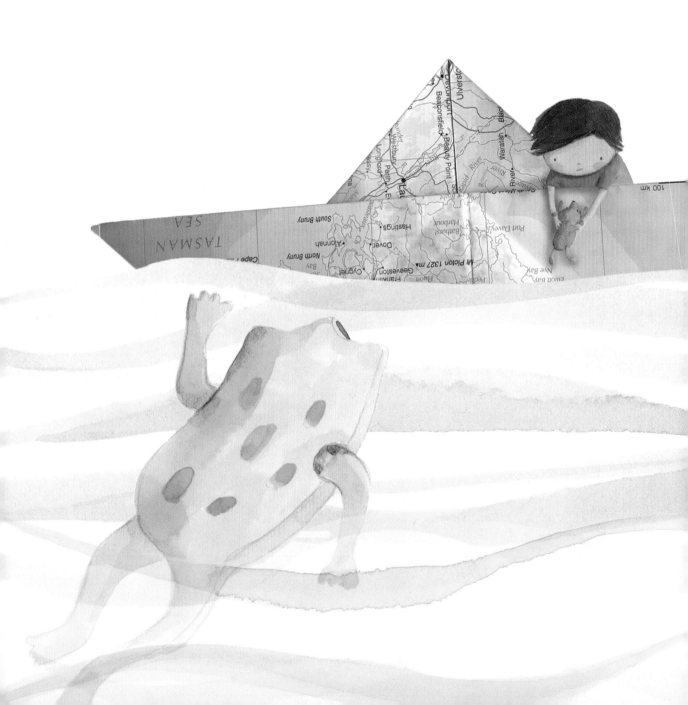

which was guarded
by fearsome frogs.

We sailed right into a
terrible storm . . .

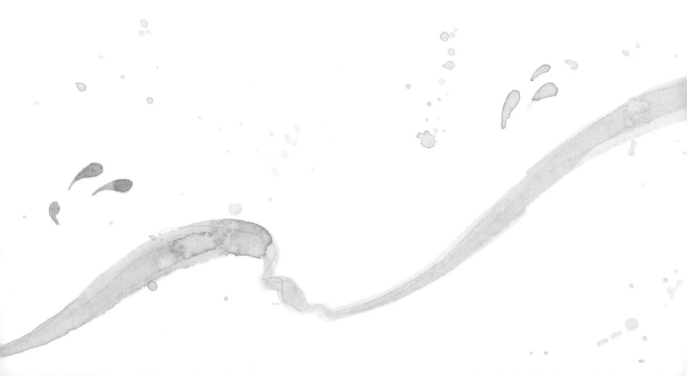

and were rescued by

a huge whale . . .

who threw us high into the air!

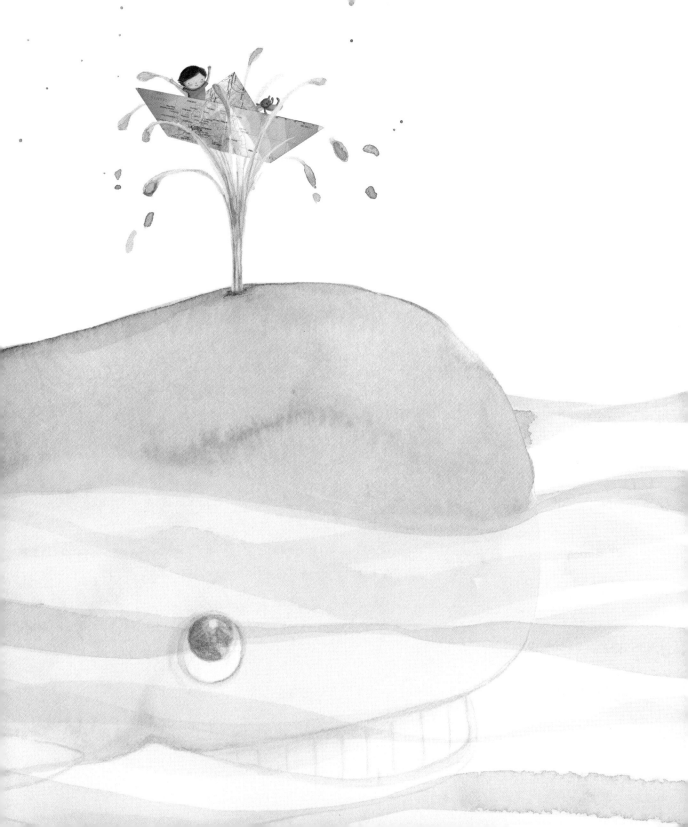

We landed in a
swirling whirlpool.

We went around and
around and around.

But luckily we
were saved.

Just in time for bed.

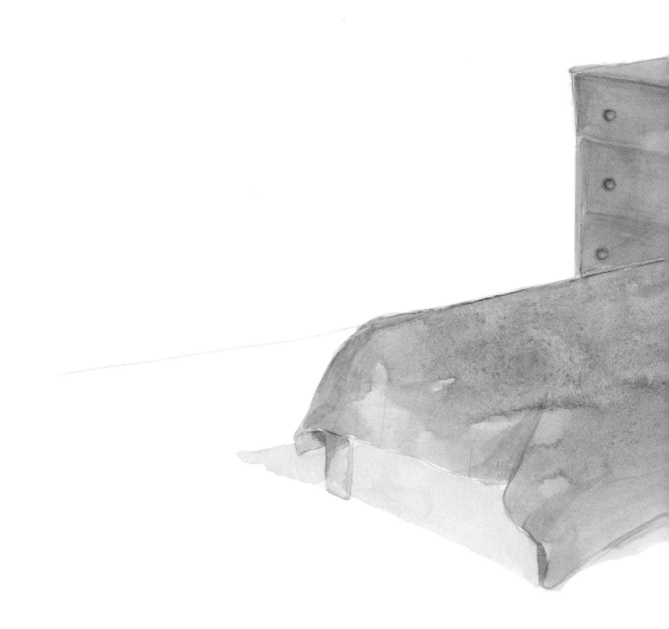

Good night.

How to make a little boat

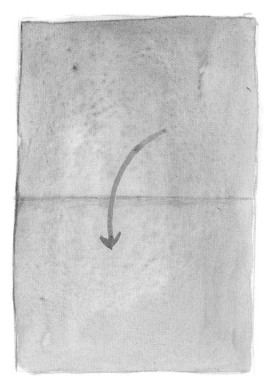

1. Fold a rectangular piece of paper in half.

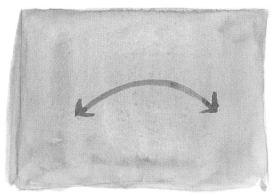

2. Fold it in half again, then unfold it.

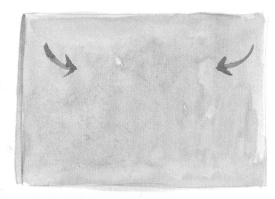

3. Fold the top corners to the center.

4. Fold the bottom strip upward.

5. Turn the paper over, and fold the other bottom strip upward.

6. Unflatten the boat to make a cone. On each side, tuck one of the bottom-strip corners under the other. Flatten the boat to form a square.

9. Push the bottom corners together, and reflatten the shape into a square.

7. Take one lower corner of the square, and fold it upward.

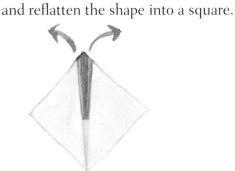

10. Grab the upper corners, and pull them apart to pop up your little boat!

8. Turn the square over, and repeat.

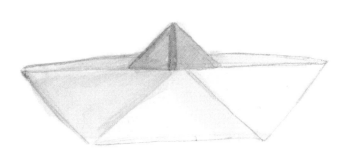